D1670055

LÓRÁND HEGYI

ANGELIKA THOMAS JAKOB DE CHIRICO

“MAKELA”

Kommentar zum analogischen Denken

Angelika Thomas und Jakob De Chirico

Hinter den Performances und Installationen, Objekten und Texten von Jakob De Chirico und Angelika Thomas ist ein heroischer Eroberungskampf um die ursprüngliche - hypothetische - Einheit von Subjekt und Objekt, Erde und Himmel, Banalität und Transzendenz, Arbeit und Kult verborgen. "Als Himmel und Erde noch nicht waren" - schrieben sie zu einer Performance im Jahr 1990, wobei die Klassifikation der Kunstgattung als "rituelle Aktion" sehr verräterisch ist. Ritus ist das Vehikulum, die Methode, um die nicht mehr kohärenten Existenzerfahrungen mit ihren Reflexionen zur Einheit zu bringen. "Aktion", das alte und ewig aktuelle Zauberwort des aktivistischen Prinzips der Avantgarde, welches die Diskrepanz zwischen Wahrheit der Kunst und sozialer Realität des Kunstproduktes als integrierbarem Gegenstand aufzulösen versucht, wird hier als Zentralbegriff verstanden. Die "Aktion" ist eine Möglichkeit für den Künstler eine "ästhetische Korrektur" durchzuführen, die die Welt der quasi-rationalistischen, banal-alltäglichen, borniert-zweckgebundenen Determination zu verändern versucht, um eine geistige Totalität der existenziellen Reflexionen und archetypischen Existenzerfahrungen zu schaffen. Die "Aktion" ist ein Versuch die analytischen Prozesse zu einem katartisch-elementaren Prozess zu verändern, wobei uralte, von kulturgeschichtlichen Konnotationen und Symbolen belastete Bedeutungsebenen "revitalisiert" und "mobilisiert" werden. In diesem Zusammenhang könnte man feststellen, daß die "Aktion" ständig versucht nicht nur eine ästhetisch-ethische "Konkurrenz" zum Leben, sondern auch eine vollkommene Ersetzung des Lebens zu sein. Die Aktionskunst baut eine Brücke zwischen Realität (also "Ist-Zustand") und Projekt (also "ideale", "fiktive" Totalität, sinnvolle Komplexität und erfaßbare Vollkommenheit unterschiedlichster Elemente); und eben dadurch ist die Aktionskunst eine ästhetische Waffe der radikalen Avantgarde, die heute ihre Position völlig neu bestimmen, und ihr Verhältnis zur Utopie völlig neu definieren muß.

Während die 20er Jahre noch mit einer - historisch verständlichen-Naivität und mit einem jakobinischen Illusionismus diese geschaffene Totalität betrachtet haben - als ethischer Imperativus, als kompromißlos herstellbare "geistige Realität" der Möglichkeiten - sind die Künstler der 80er und 90er Jahre viel distanzierter und skeptischer: Heute versucht man die Utopie als Metapher zu interpretieren, mit der Konsequenz der kulturgeschichtlichen Dimension, das heißt, mit der Analogie. Das analogische Denken ermöglicht dem Künstler unterschiedliche Zeichensysteme, verschiedene Wertvorstellungen, Sprachen, Philosophien und rituelle Praktiken als "Hilfsmaterial" zu reaktivieren, ohne irgendein System zu absolutieren.
Kultur als Metapher des Systems; Ritus als Analogie der Existenzerfahrung.
Einerseits zeigt die Ritus-Auffassung von Jakob De Chirico und Angelika Thomas einen "enzyklopädischen" Charakter auf, andererseits ist eine radikale "nihilistische" Haltung prägnant präsent - oft in Form einer kulturkritischen In-Frage-Stellung konventioneller Wertesysteme und scheinbar relevanter Zusammenhänge.
Der "enzyklopädische" Charakter bezieht sich auf die Nebeneinanderstellung und "Inventarisierung" der unterschiedlichsten kultischen Prozesse, Zeichensprachen, Symbole und Hinweise auf rituelle Praktiken, die in den Performances durch eine Dramaturgie des Geschehens, beziehungsweise durch eine Dramaturgie des Aufzählens erscheinen, und zur erfassbaren, wahrnehmbaren Form umgestaltet werden. Diese spezifische "Inventarisierung" selbst wird als Ritus dargestellt; das heißt, die Aktion der Aufzählung und der Nebeneinanderstellung bekommt eine ästhetische Form, die sich in dem zeitlichen Ablauf des Geschehens, also in der Dramaturgie der Aktion, manifestiert. Die Zeitgebundenheit des konkreten Geschehens betont eben die Zeitlosigkeit des Ritus, also die Transzendenz. Dieser scheinbare Widerspruch "befreit" die Aktion von der pseudo-wissenschaftlichen

Objektivität der Inventarisierung, die aus Beispielen und Zitaten besteht, und öffnet einen freien Raum für die poetisch-metaphorischen Assoziationen, welche die im zeitlichen Ablauf sich entfaltenden ästhetischen Formen zur sinnlich-konkreten Metapher existentieller Erfahrungen umdeuten. Dieser zeitlich lange Ablauf verleiht den Performances von De Chirico und Thomas einen archaischen Charakter, obwohl sie nie direkt mit den Methoden der ästhetischen Archaisierung operieren. Archaisch bedeutet hier die Monumentalität der dargestellten Aktionen, Bewegungen, "Arbeitsprozesse" (wie z.B. das Tragen verschiedener Gegenstände, das Vorbereiten der kommenden Aktionen und Taten, oder das Aufstellen und Aufbauen der "Installationen"), die keine ästhetische Kosmetik, keine Verschönerung oder kein Verbergen erlaubt. Archaisch wirkt auch der Zusammenhang zwischen menschlichem Körper (als "Arbeitsgerät", als Gegenstand, als Vehikulum) und dem gebauten, gemachten, geformten Gegenstand materieller Substanz. Aber auch unter diesem Aspekt kann man über keine Archaisierung sprechen: Die Beziehung zwischen Körper und Gegenstand ist mehr objektiv, sachlich, zweckmäßig logisch und unpersönlich als romantisch archaisierend im Sinne der ästhetisch-poetischen Formsprache. De Chirico und Thomas versuchen die Formsprache als solche zu vergessen, um eine Direktheit und archaische Objektivität gewinnen zu können. Zu dieser Objektivität gehört die langsame, konsequente Aufzählung der kultischen Praktiken, als Methode des metaphorischen Bewußtmachens, welches nur im Bereich der künstlerischen "radikalen Fiktion" möglich ist.
Die in den letzten zwei Jahren fertiggestellten Objekte von Jakob De Chirico und Angelika Thomas zeigen in ihrem Gefüge verborgene Ähnlichkeiten mit den zeitlichen Strukturen der Performances und rituellen Aktionen: Das zeitliche "Nacheinandersein" wurde durch das räumliche "Nebeneinandersein" ersetzt. Beide Modelle bauen sich auf durch die Aufzählung nacheinander kommender - oder nebeneinander

stehender - “zentrischer Einheiten”, welche sich immer um ein spirituelles Zentrum organisieren, jedoch ihre eigentliche Bedeutung eben in der Form der “objektiven” und “sachlichen” Nebeneinanderstellung bekommen. So entsteht - fast ohne evidente Intervention der Künstler- die Monumentalität der Tatsachen, die eine Zeitlosigkeit und archaische Objektivität, Unabsichtlichkeit manifestiert.
Da liegt ein zweiter Widerspruch: Die Kontradiktion zwischen den - immer mit “symbolisch-metaphorischen” Elementen dargestellten - spirituellen Zentren, und den spontanen, anarchistischen, unabsichtlich gesammelten und aufgehäuften Gegenständen. Diese zwei, miteinander konfrontierten Momente repräsentieren zwei unterschiedliche Wertvorstellungen, bzw. zwei ästhetische Attitüden, die auch zwei Modernistische Traditionen reaktivieren: Die symbolisch-metaphysisch-surrealistische und die dadaistisch-neorealistisch-aktionistische Tradition. Jakob De Chirico und Angelika Thomas lassen sich einen ziemlich breiten Spielraum öffnen, wobei die unterschiedlichen Zeichensysteme und Referenzkontexte sich miteinander vermischen. So bekommt ihr Oeuvre einerseits einen historischen Aspekt (durch die kunstgeschichtlichen Referenzen), andererseits eine betonte und unauflösbare Zeitlosigkeit (durch die Monotonie der Wiederholung der Gegenstände und “ritueller” Aktionen).
Jakob De Chirico und Angelika Thomas versuchen die Gegenstände in einen Kontext der rituell-spirituellen Zusammenhänge zurückzubringen, ohne eine einseitige und anakronistisch mystifizierte Pseudo-Archaisierung auf der Ebene der künstlerischen Formsprache zu verwirklichen; der Ritus wird hier als Metapher (als ästhetisches Mittel) interpretiert, welcher eine mögliche Komplexität der unterschiedlichen Bedeutungsebenen und Erfahrungsbereiche modelliert. Diese unterschiedlichen Erfahrungsebenen werden hier als Materialien des Bewußtmachens präsentiert. Das Bewußtmachen als Analogie der künstlerischen Tätigkeit verbindet die historischen Konnotationen mit der Zeitlosigkeit des ewigen Wiederholens; die Zeitgebundenheit der Aktion wird durch die “rituelle Aktion” der archaischen Vollkommenheit relativiert. Pathos und Relativierung, Ritus und “ad hocism”, Hierarchie und Chaos manifestieren die extremen Pole der Kunst von Jakob De Chirico und Angelika Thomas.

Lóránd Hegyi
Palais Liechtenstein
Museum Moderner Kunst, Stiftung Ludwig
Wien

“MAKELA”

Format der Arbeiten	
Misure dei lavori	*110 x 90 cm*
Size of Works	

1

2

3

4

65

6

7

8

Der Eisenhimmel ist der gedruckte Schaltkreis um die Sternschnuppen einzufangen.

Il cielo di lamiere è il circuito stampato per le stelle cadenti.

The iron sky is the printed circuit capturing shooting stars.

10

12

14

16

18

20

SPORT

22

SPOBS TZ

Die genetische Erbanlage der Materie reproduziert auf der Fibonacci-Schiene die Räume der Evolution.

Sulla rotaia di Fibonacci l'eredità genetica della materia ricalca gli spazi dell'evoluzione.

The genetically inherited tendencies of matter reproduce the spaces of evolution on the Fibonacci track.

24

1974027M
ALITALIA
PROPERTY
TOP
DESSUS
NUCA

832040

28

30

32

34

36

Commento al pensiero analogico
Angelika Thomas & Jakob De Chirico

Dietro le performances e le installazioni, gli oggetti ed i testi di Angelica Thomas e Jakob De Chirico, si cela un'eroica lotta tesa alla conquista dell'unità primordiale - ipotetica - tra soggetto ed oggetto, terra e cielo, banalità e trascendenza, lavoro e culto. " Quando cielo e terra ancora non esistevano" scrissero nel 1990 per una loro performance, accanto alla quale la classificazione del genere artistico come "azione rituale" è alquanto rivelatrice. Rito è il veicolo, il metodo per riportare le esperienze esistenziali non più coerenti ad unità con le loro riflessioni. "Azione", l'antica ed eternamente attuale parola magica del principio attivo dell'avanguardia, che tenta di dissolvere la discrepanza tra realtà artistica e realtà sociale del prodotto artistico - inteso come oggetto integrabile - viene qui posta come concetto centrale.
L' "azione" é una possibilità per l'artista di attuare una "correzione estetica" che tenta di trasformare il mondo della determinazione pseudo-razionale, banal-quotidiana, ottuso-funzionale, per creare una totalità spirituale di riflessi esistenziali e di esperienze esistenziali archetipe. L'"azione" è un tentativo di trasformazione dei processi analitici in un processo catartico elementare, "rivitalizzando" e "mobilitando" antichissimi livelli di significati schiacciati dal peso di connotazioni e simboli storico-culturali. In questo contesto si potrebbe prendere atto del fatto che l'azione non solo tenta ininterrottamente di essere una concorrente etico-estetica della vita, ma anche una sua totale sostituzione. L'arte di azione getta un ponte tra la realtà (cioè la "condizione che è") ed il progetto (cioé la totalità "ideale", "fittizia", la complessità significante e la perfezione tangibile dei più diversi elementi); ed appunto per ciò l'arte di azione è un'arma estetica dell'avanguardia radicale, che oggi deve ridefinire in modo del tutto nuovo la propria posizione ed il proprio raporto nei confronti dell'utopia.
Mentre gli anni 20 vedevano questa totalità inventata ancora con

un'ingenuità - storicamente comprensibile - e con un illusionismo giacobino - come imperativo etico, come "realtà spirituale" delle possibilità, realizzabile senza compromessi - gli artisti degli anni 80 e 90 sono più distaccati e scettici: oggi si cerca di interpretare l'utopia come metafora, con il risultato della dimensione storico-culturale, ciò significa con l'analogia. Il pensiero analogico permette all'artista di riattivare come "materiale di supporto" differenti sistemi segnici, concezioni di valori, linguaggi, filosofie e pratiche rituali diverse, senza assolutizzare alcun sistema.

Cultura come metafora del sistema; rito come analogia dell'esperienza esistenziale.

Per un verso la concezione del rito da parte di Angelica Thomas e Jakob De Chirico evidenzia un carattere "enciclopedico", per l'altro è presente in modo pregnante una radicale posizione "nichilista" - spesso sotto forma di critica culturale e di messa in discussione dei sistemi di valori convenzionali e dei collegamenti solo apparentemente rilevanti.

Il carattere "enciclopedico" si riferisce all'accostamento ed all' "annotazione" dei diversi procedimenti cultici, linguaggi segnici, simboli e riferimenti a pratiche rituali, che nelle performances appaiono attraverso una drammaturgia dell'evento, o meglio attraverso una drammaturgia dell'inventario e vengono tramutate in forma tangibile e percepibile. Questo stesso specifico "inventariare" viene rappresentato come rito; ciò vuol dire che l'azione di annotare ed accostare riceve una forma estetica, che si manifesta nello svolgersi dell'evento nel tempo, cioé nella drammaturgia dell'azione. Il legame dell'avvenimento concreto con il tempo rimarca appunto l'assenza di tempo nel rito, cioé la trascendenza. Questa apparente contraddizione "libera" l'azione dall'oggettività pseudoscientifica dell'inventariare, fatta di esempi e citazioni, ed apre uno spazio libero alle associazioni poetico-metaforiche, che tramutano il significato delle

forme estetiche che si sviluppano in sequenza temporale, nella metafora concreto-sensibile delle esperienze esistenziali. Questo decorso per tempi lunghi conferisce alle performances di Thomas e De Chirico un carattere arcaico, per quanto essi non operino mai direttamente con i metodi dell'arcaicizzazione estetica. Arcaico significa qui monumentalità delle azioni rappresentate, dei movimenti, dei "procedimenti lavorativi" (come per esempio il trasporto di diversi oggetti, la preparazione delle azioni e dei fatti imminenti o l'impianto e la costruzione delle "installazioni") che non consente alcuna cosmesi estetica, alcun abbellimento o velatura. Arcaico è anche l'effetto prodotto dal rapporto tra il corpo umano (come "strumento di lavoro", come oggetto, come veicolo) e l'oggetto costruito, fatto, forgiato nella sostanza materiale. Ma nemmeno sotto questo aspetto si può parlare di arcaicizzazione: il rapporto tra corpo ed oggetto è piuttosto concreto, reale, funzionalmente logico ed impersonale, non tanto arcaicizzante in senso romantico come lo intende il linguaggio delle forme poetico-estetiche. Thomas e De Chirico cercano di scordare il linguaggio delle forme come tale per poter guadagnare un'immediatezza ed un'oggettività arcaica. Fa parte di questa oggettività il lento, pignolo conteggio delle pratiche cultiche, quale metodo per dare consapevolezza attraverso la metafora, cosa possibile solo nel campo artistico della "finzione radicale".
Gli oggetti realizzati da Angelika Thomas e Jakob De Chirico negli ultimi due anni celano nella loro struttura evidenti somiglianze con le compagini temporali delle performances e delle azioni rituali: la "consecutio" temporale è stata sostituita dall' "accostamento" spaziale. Entrambi i modelli prendono corpo attraverso l'enumerazione di "unità centrali" - in successione o in accostamento - che si organizzano sempre attorno ad un centro spirituale; acquistano comunque il loro particolare significato proprio nella forma dell'accostamento "oggettivo" e "concreto". Così ha origine - quasi senza mani-

festo intervento da parte dell'artista - la monumentalità dei fatti, che esprime assenza di tempo, oggettività arcaica ed involontarietà.
Qui sta una seconda contraddizione: la contrapposizione tra i centri spirituali - rappresentati sempre per mezzo di elementi "simbolico-metaforici" - e gli oggetti spontanei, anarchici, raccolti ed accumulati senza intenzionalità. Questi due momenti, confrontati tra loro, rappresentano due diverse concezioni di valori o meglio due atteggiamenti estetici, che riattivano anche due tradizioni modernistiche: la tradizione simbolico-metafisica-surrealista e quella dadaista-neorealista-azionista. Angelika Thomas e Jakob De Chirico si lasciano aperto un campo d'azione alquanto vasto, che permette ai diversi sistemi segnici ed ai contesti di riferimento di mescolarsi tra loro. La loro opera acquista così per un verso un aspetto storico (attraverso riferimenti alla storia dell'arte), per l'altro verso, un carattere atemporale rimarcato ed insolubile (attraverso la monotonia della ripetizione degli oggetti e delle azioni "rituali").
Angelika Thomas e Jakob De Chirico cercano di riportare gli oggetti in un contesto di relazioni rituali-spirituali, evitando di produrre sul piano del linguaggio artistico delle forme una pseudo-arcaicizzazione limitante e mistificante in senso anacronistico; il rito viene interpretato come metafora (come mezzo estetico), che modella una possibile complessità dei diversi livelli di significati e campi d'esperienza. Questi diversi livelli di esperienza vengono qui presentati come materiali che portano a consapevolezza. Dare coscienza inteso come analogia dell'attività artistica, collega i caratteri storici con l'assenza di tempo dell'eterno ripetere; la temporalità dell'azione viene relativata attraverso la perfezione arcaica dell' "azione rituale". Rito e "ad hoc-ismo", gerarchia e caos evidenziano i poli estremi dell'arte di Angelika Thomas e Jakob De Chirico.

Lóránd Hegyi
Palais Liechtenstein
Museum Moderner Kunst, Stiftung Ludwig
Vienna

38

39

40

122
001
604

44

46

Die Venusbilder, auf den Häuten der Bäume in den Regenbogenfarben tätowiert, emittieren den in den 50' er Jahren aufgeladenen Orgon.

Le Veneri tatuate sulle pelli degli alberi nei colori dell'arcobaleno sprigionano l'orgon caricato negli anni '50.

The images of Venus tattooed in the colors of the rainbow on the skin of the trees emit the orgone dammed up in the Fifties.

UNIE
Frankfurter
ranke
hen
ann man
eilen
omântik
m Elbrus
ONEM
NNE
S
ALLS

48

DA 81
COMPLETI
CAPACITÀ

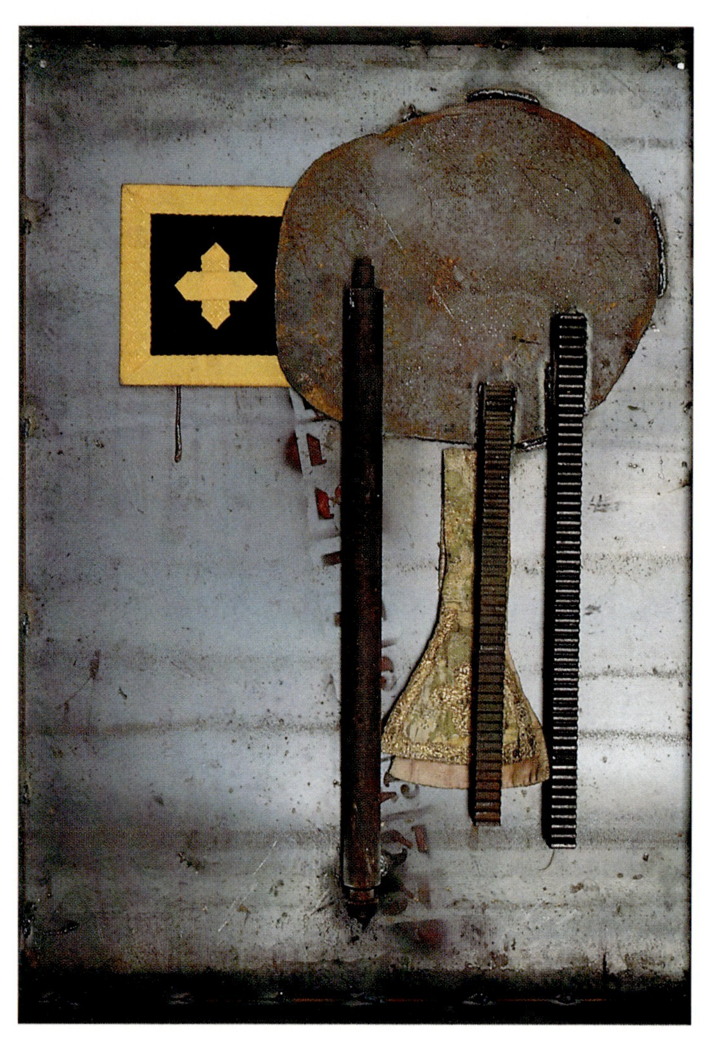

50

IL MONDO DI DOMANI

MORTAIO DA 81
3 COLPI COMPLETI
PICCOLA CAPACITÀ
MORTAIO DA 81
3 COLPI COMPLETI
A PICCOLA CAPACITÀ
75025

52

54

56

9
76

58

Auf dem haitianischen Vévé spalten sich die Zeiten des Geistes von den Zeiten der Dinge.

Sul ve-ve haitiano i tempi dello spirito si scollano dai tempi delle cose.

The time of the spirit and the time of material things diverge on the Haitian vévé.

60

1/3

62

a un anno
di Pio XII

64

66

1346269

68

Bauknecht
MAGGI

96258854
105
435671
200 CARTRIDGES
7.62MM NATO M80
CARTONS M13

72

Notes on the Analogical Thinking
of Angelika Thomas and Jakob De Chirico

The installations, objects and texts of Angelika Thomas and Jakob De Chirico are grounded in an heroic struggle to reacquire the primordial — even if hypothetical — unity of subject and object, earth and sky, banality and transcendence, work and religious ritual. One remembers that a performance they created in 1990 was flanked by the phrase "When the earth and the sky did not yet exist." And the specification of the genre of art to which this performance belonged described it, significantly enough, as a "ritual action." Ritual is the vehicle or method these artists adopt in their attempt to deal with disorderly existential experience and to assign it a place in their reflections. But the central concept, here, is "action" — that magical word, both ancient and always up-to-date, that sums up the active principle of the ways in which the avantgardes have attempted to eliminate the discrepancy between the artistic and social realities of the work of art.

"Actions" offer the artist a possibility to effect an "aesthetic correction" that serves to transform our perception of our pseudo-rational, banally quotidian and obtusely functional world, and thus to enter the sphere of a spiritual whole that can deal with the archetypes of existential experience. "Actions" constitute an attempt to transform the modes of analytic thought into a cathartic and elementary process that "mobilizes" and "revitalizes" ancient levels of meaning that have come to be crushed beneath the weight of historical circumstance and established cultural symbol. Actions, from such a point of view, do even something more than posit themselves as ceaseless attempts to compete with life on the ethical and aesthetic plane; they are committed to its total replacement. Art that takes the form of actions throws a bridge between reality ("the condition that is") and possible project (the "ideal" or "fictive" totality that reveals the complex meanings and tangible perfection of all of its most disparate parts); and that precisely is the reason why "action art" presents itself as one of the principle aesthetic weapons of the radical avantgarde, which today has to set its sights on a complete and wholly new reformulation of the ways in which it relates to utopian ideals.

The artists of the 1920s dealt with such notions of fictive or invented totality in ways that remained naive — or in terms, to be fair, of a naiveté that itself was historically determined — and their Jacobean illusions conferred it with the status of an ethical imperative. The "spiritual reality" of envisioned possibilities seemed to allow for no

compromise in their effective realization. The artists of the 1980s and 1990s are more detached and skeptical. Utopia today has the quality of a metaphor. It is seen to interact with historical and cultural circumstance, and it serves for purposes of analogy. Analogical thinking gives access to a wide variety of "materials" — systems of signs, concepts of value, diverse languages, philosophies and ritual practices — that the artist can proceed to "activate" while never conferring any one of them with the status an absolute.
Culture serves as the metaphor of the whole of the system in which we live; ritual is seen as analogous to existential experience.
The concept of ritual as employed by Angelika Thomas and Jakob De Chirico shows, on the one hand, an "encyclopedic" character; on the other, it is clearly imbued with radically "nihilist" attitudes. It is charged with cultural criticism and questions our systems of conventional values and only apparent communication.
The "encyclopedic" character of their rites is revealed in the juxtaposition and "annotation" of the various symbols, languages of signs, cult procedures, and references to ritual practices that appear in their performances in terms of a kind of dramatization of the event itself, or, more precisely, through a dramatization of the making of such inventories, thus coming to find themselves endowed with tangible and perceptible form. The making of inventories is itself presented as a rite. This is to say that the action of making notations and creating juxtapositions takes on an aesthetic form that comes to manifestation as the event unfolds in time, assuming its character as theatrical action. The way in which the event finds concrete articulation in time underlines the fact of the absence of time in ritual itself, which is to speak of the transcendence of ritual. This apparent contradiction frees the action from the pseudo-scientific objectivity of its making of inventories, which consist of examples and quotes, and it opens up a space for poetic or metaphoric associations that transform the presence of the aesthetic forms, as they appear in temporal sequence, into a concrete and sense-perceptible metaphor of existential experience. The way in which the performances of Thomas and De Chirico take place in the course of extended periods of time gives them a somehow archaic character, even though the artists never work directly with methods of aesthetic archaicization. What makes this work feel archaic is the sheer monumentality of the actions it presents, or of the movements and procedures

involved (such as ways in which various objects are carried back and forth, or the making of preparations for actions and facts that are soon to take place, or the setting up and construction of the "installations.") The process allows no room for aesthetic embellishment; nothing can be beautified and nothing can be concealed. There is also something archaic in the relationship between the human body (as "tool," as object, as vehicle) and the substance of the material objects that come to be made, forged, or constructed. But here again it proves impossible to talk about intentional archaicization. Rather than archaicizing in any romantic sense that depends on a language of poetic and aesthetic forms, the relationship that holds between the body and the object is real, concrete, logically functional, and quite impersonal. Thomas and De Chirico attempt to pay no attention to the language of forms as such so as better to achieve a sense of immediacy, and thus of something objectively archaic. A part of this sense of the objectively archaic derives from the slow, meticulous recitation of various cult practices; these forms of recitation themselves come to constitute a method for the creation of awareness through metaphor, which is something that art finds possible only through the use of devices of "radical fiction." The structure of the objects that Angelika Thomas and Jakob De Chirico have realized in the course of the last two years can also be seen to be related to the temporal aspects of the artists' ritual performances and actions. The use of temporal "sequences" is replaced by spatial "juxtapositions." But in both of these cases we are dealing with models that assume their form through the enumeration of "central units" than organize themselves — no matter if as sequences or as juxtapositions — around a spiritual center. We are dealing here with objects that discover their particular meaning in "objective" and "concrete" juxtapositions. And this is what accounts — nearly in the absence of all manifest intervention on the part of the artists themselves — for the monumentality of the facts with which they present us; and it is precisely that sense of monumentality that speaks of the absence of time, of the objectively archaic, and of things that happen on their own, independently of anyone's will. Here we discover a second contradiction: the contrast between the spiritual centers — always represented through elements of symbol and metaphor — and the spontaneous, anarchical objects that have been collected and accumulated without any sense of intention or

specific purpose. These two moments, confronted the one with the other, correspond to two different concepts of value, or to two aesthetic attitudes that also reactivate two different aspects of modern art history: the symbolist, metaphysical and surrealist tradition on the one hand, and the dada, new realist, and actionist tradition on the other. Angelika Thomas and Jakob De Chirico allow themselves access to quite a considerable range of action, thus permitting the interpenetration of various systems of signs and diverse frames of reference. Their work thus sites itself in history (through references to the history of art) while nonetheless remaining insistently and irreversibly atemporal (through a monotonous repetition of "ritual" objects and actions.)
Angelika Thomas and Jakob De Chirico attempt to reinsert their objects into a context of ritualistic and spiritual relationships, but they do so while avoiding any language of artistic forms that would simply imitate archaic modes of thought in limited, mystified, or anachronistic ways. Ritual is understood as a metaphor (as aesthetic means) that reaches out to a possible complexity of diverse levels of meaning and fields of experience. Such diverse levels of experience are themselves experienced as materials that give access to awareness. The creation of consciousness — which in turn is a metaphor of artistic activity — reconnects historical fact to a sense of eternal return that lies outside of time. The temporality of the artists' actions finds itself relativized by the archaic perfection that's a part of their presence as "ritual action." The poles of the art of Angelika Thomas and Jakob De Chirico are to be found in their sense of ritual on the one hand, and in their sense of the *ad hoc* on the other — in hierarchy, no less than in chaos.

Lóránd Hegyi
Palais Liechtenstein
Museum Moderner Kunst, Stiftung Ludwig
Vienna

(Translation: Henry Martin)

5 2 7 9
3 9 6
9 1 9 8 4 6
5 7

74

78

6394598

80

82

591
879

Die Reise der Gegenstände projiziert sich auf die Wiederfindung einer virtuellen Seele.

Il viaggio degli oggetti si proietta verso il recupero di un'anima virtuale.

The objects' voyage projects itself toward the rediscovery of an intangible soul.

84

196418

86

88

GERALDINE CHAPLIN

1 4 7
1 3
101

3 7 8 8 9 0 6 2 5 7
3 1 4 5 9 0 6

92

94

In der Feuertaufe entflieht die evozierte DNA dem Labyrinth um sich in der neuen Konfiguration zu materialisieren.

Nel battesimo del fuoco il DNA evocato si libera dal labirinto per materializzarsi nella nuova costellazione.

Through the baptism in fire the evoked DNA escapes the labyrinth and materializes in the new configuration.

DARE
Magazzino
Olio
AVERE

7778742049

100

80
80 67194370
80
81
61
20
200 CARTRIDGES
NATO 7.62MM, LINKED
CARTONS, BANDOLEERS
1 TR M62 - 4 BALL M80
FUNC LOT RA L 85097

102

46368

wird

108

14930352

110

112

W
IL SINDAC
Marco Mag

ANGELIKA THOMAS
geboren 1955 in Aachen
Studium der Diplom-Biologie
Ausbildung als Schauspielerin
ab 1986 Performance, Rauminstallationen
ab 1987 Eisenskulpturen, Objekte

JAKOB DE CHIRICO
geboren 1943 in Innsbruck
1968 Diplom der Kunstschule St. Ulrich (Gröden)
1973 Diplom der Kunstakademie München
ab 1954 eigene Arbeiten, zahlreiche Einzel-und Gruppenausstellungen, u.a.
1982 «Centre Pompidou», Paris
1986 «Dokumenta, K 18», Kassel

GEMEINSAME ARBEITEN AB 1988 (AUSWAHL)

AKTIONEN

1988 Trento, «Kut Kilgarugi»
München, «Gri Gri Vé Vé»
1989 München, Galerie der Künstler, «Odem I»
Cavriago, Centro della Performance, «Odem II»
Bozen, «Ouroborus»
1990 München, Olympiagelände Süd, «Einfrierung»
Vinschgau, Rimpf Höfe, «Tombolo: Franziskus, Ben und Clara»
Köln, Moltkerei Werkstatt, «Power & Spass für I. Kümmel»
1991 München, Atelierhaus Klenzestrasse Souterrain, «Rapina I»
Illasi/Verona, Domus Jani, «Rapina II»
Mira/Venedig, Villa dei Leoni, «Senza titolo»
München, Gasteig, «Colombo»
1992 Berlin, Künstlerhaus Bethanien,
«Makela - 1 Trog Wein = 1 Mensch»
Bozen, Circolo Masetti, «Crocifrittura»
Castelfranco Veneto, «Domino»
1993 München, Praterinsel, «Aus der Nigredo zur DNA der Prima Materia».

AUSSTELLUNGEN

1988 Albisola, Galleria Balestrini, «Totem»
Sella di Borgo, Arte Sella, «Hexenküche»
1989 Berlin, Akademie der Künste
München, Künstlerwerkstatt Lothringerstrasse,
«Ressource Kunst», «Das Bett des Phönix»
1990 München, Zollhalle, «Bogen und Erbse»
Budapest, Mücsarnok, «Ressource Kunst»
«Kreuzung»
Reggio Emilia, Edizioni Pari & Dispari, «Samthandschuhe»
1991 Atelierhaus Klenzestrasse Souterrain,
«Triangolo 4»
München, Atelierhaus Klenzestrasse Souterrain,
«Im Monat des Regenbogens»
München, Café Größenwahn, «Wirtshauskunst»
Verona, Edizioni Adriano Parise, «$E = mc^2$»,
(mit Ugo Dossi)
Illasi/Verona, Domus Jani, «Makela»
1992 München, Atelierhaus Klenzestrasse Souterrain, «Fuoribordo»
Genova, Museo attivo delle forme inconsapevoli, «Evocare Colombo»
Capri, Casa Malaparte, Edizioni Pari & Dispari, «Zukunst»
München, Atelierhaus Klenzestrasse Souterrain, Praterinsel, «Museo attivo delle forme inconsapevoli»
1993 München, Galerie Waßermann, «115 DNA für 1001 Nacht»

PREISE

Förderpreis der Stadt München 1989
Prinzregent-Luitpold Stiftung 1990

ADRIANO PARISE
37030 COLOGNOLA AI COLLI (VR)
Tel. (045) 7650373-7650629 - Fax (045) 6150544